# Lionel Lion's
# New Car

Lionel Lion the Mayor was the most important person in
FABULAND. But even important people sometimes
have problems, as you will find out in this story.
It all began one morning, as Lionel was driving to the
Town Hall for a special meeting...

5

Lionel was in a hurry this morning. He was driving his car faster than usual, through the streets of FABULAND. "I mustn't be late," said Lionel, looking at his watch. "Clear the road!" he shouted, honking his horn. "I must get to the meeting on time."

Suddenly, there was a loud BANG.
Lionel's radiator was squirting water and the tyres were
beginning to hiss. And there was a loud knocking noise
coming from the engine.
Something was very wrong.

Lionel stopped the car and jumped out. He was furious. Just then, Police Chief Bertie Bulldog came along on his motorcycle.

"You can't park there," said Bertie, getting out his notebook. Then he saw it was the Mayor.

"Er, sorry," said Bertie. "Is anything the matter?"

"Everything!" roared Lionel. "Just look at my car. Send for Billy Bear at once."

Billy owned a garage and knew all about mending cars.

Police Chief Bertie rode off to Billy's garage as fast as
he could. The Mayor was in no mood to be kept waiting.
"Quick, Billy," said Bertie when he got to the garage.
"Lionel's car has broken down. You had better bring
your tow truck."
"I'll come straightaway," said Billy.

By the time Bertie and Billy arrived, Lionel was looking
crosser than ever.
"Please hurry up and mend my car," said Lionel.
He waved some important-looking papers in the air.
"We are discussing the plans for the Town Hall roof
garden today and I musn't be late."

Billy looked at the Mayor's car. It was a wreck.
"I can't mend this," said Billy. "You ought to buy
a new car."
"A new car!" roared Lionel. "I haven't got time to go out
and buy a new car. I am much too busy."
"Well," said Billy. "I could make you one. What sort of
car would you like?"

Lionel thought for a moment.
Then he borrowed Ricky's pencil and drew a car
very quickly on a piece of paper.
"There," said Lionel, handing the paper to Billy. "Make
me a car like that as soon as you can."

12

Police Chief Bertie suggested that he should take Lionel
to the Town Hall on his motorcycle.
"Thank you," said Lionel. "If we hurry, I shall be
in time for the special meeting."

13

Billy folded Lionel's drawing and put it in his pocket.
He was going to look at it carefully later on.
"Well," said Billy. "I had better get busy and hitch
this wreck on to the back of my tow truck."
Billy hitched the front bumper of Lionel's old car on
to his special towing hook.

Then he towed the car back to the garage.
At the garage, Morty Mouse was leaning against the petrol
pumps having a quiet snooze. Morty sometimes helped Billy.
"Wake up!" cried Billy. "There's work to be done. Take
this old car to bits. When you've finished, you can help
me build the Mayor's new car."
Poor Morty.
It sounded like a lot of hard work.

Billy Bear took Lionel's drawing out of his pocket and studied it. Billy looked puzzled.
He had never seen a car quite like it.
"I have seen a lot of cars," he said. "But this is the strangest one of all."
However, the Mayor's orders had to be obeyed and Billy set to work immediately.

First, Billy collected all the things he needed to build
the new car.
Windows, wheels and seats. Bumpers, brakes and lights.
"Come on, Morty," cried Billy. "I need some grass and
flowers, too."
"Grass and flowers?" said Morty. "What do you need
those for?"
"The Mayor's new car, of course," said Billy. "Hurry up.
There's no time to lose."

Inside the garage, Billy and Morty worked hard all day.
Morty spent most of his time gathering flowers.
At last the car was ready.
"Open the doors, Morty," said Billy. "We'll go for a
drive to test it."

Morty was just opening the garage doors when Lionel
came along, looking very worried.
"Hello, Lionel," said Morty. "You are just in time to see
your new car."
"Never mind about my new car," said Lionel. "I have lost
the plans for the new roof garden. They were on a piece
of paper. I am sure I had them this morning when my car
broke down..."

Lionel stopped.
Billy had just driven Lionel's new car out of the garage.
What a car!
It looked more like a taxi with a garden on top.
"There you are, Lionel," said Billy. "I hope you like it."
But Lionel didn't say anything.
He stared at the car with his mouth open.
"What's the matter?" asked Morty. "Don't you like it?"

"Look," said Billy. "Here is the piece of paper with
your drawing on it. We copied it exactly."
Lionel looked at the drawing.
Then he burst out laughing.
"I have drawn my car on the same piece of paper as the
plans for the Town Hall roof garden. What a stupid
mistake. No wonder I couldn't find them."

Lionel looked at his new car again.
"But the two plans work beautifully together," he
declared. "Only the Mayor of FABULAND would have
a car like that!"
"Come on," said Billy. "Let's all go for a ride.
Then everyone can see your new car."

23

So they did.
Billy drove the new car round the town while Lionel and Morty sat in the roof garden.
Lionel began playing his accordion.
"I think this is a much better place for a roof garden," said Lionel. "Don't you agree, Morty Mouse?"

24

But Morty didn't say a word.
He had fallen sound asleep under a daisy.

# Here are some of the people who live in FABULAND

Lionel Lion
Edward Elephant
Ernie Elephant

Doctor Lucy Lamb
Henry Horse
Catherine Cat
Doctor Dog

Harry Horse
Buster Bulldog
Freddy Fox
Patricia Piglet

Roger Raccoon
Gertrude Goat
Hannah Hippopotamus
Paulette Poodle